TO MY DOG FLOC,

my family, my friends, and all
the amazing people that I have
come to know this year.

First published in 2011 by Child's Play (International) Ltd
Ashworth Road, Bridgemead, Swindon SN5 7YD UK

Published in USA by Child's Play Inc
250 Minot Avenue, Auburn, Maine 04210

Distributed in Australia by Child's Play Australia Pty Ltd
Unit 10/20 Narabang Way, Belrose, NSW 2085

Text and illustrations copyright © 2011 Marta Altés
The moral right of the author/illustrator has been asserted

ISBN 978-1-84643-417-4
L290814CPL10144174

Printed and bound in Heshan, China

9 10

A catalogue record of this book is available from the British Library

www.childs-play.com

Hi! MY NAME IS <u>NO</u>.

I'm a ~~good~~ very good boy.
I AM SO GOOD THAT
MY FAMILY IS ALWAYS
CALLING my name! :)

I help them
GET TO PLACES
FASTER.

I TASTE THEIR FOOD
before they eat,
to make SURE
that it's <u>ALL RIGHT</u>.

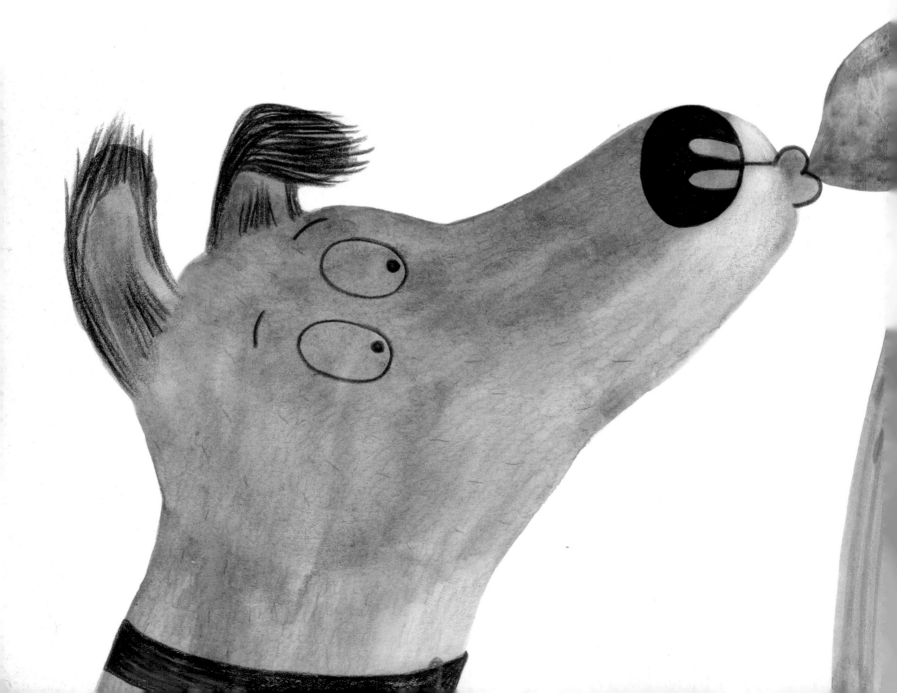

I help them
LOOK FOR treasures
IN THE GARDEN.

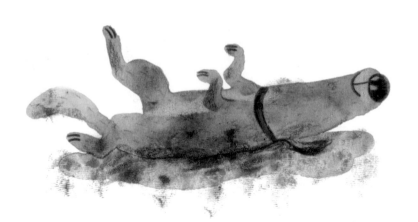

I TRY TO LOOK my best FOR THEM.

NOOOO!

I warm THEIR BEDS
BEFORE they go to sleep.

If I am hungry,
I FEED MYSELF.

I help them
WITH THE LAUNDRY.

They must
LOVE ME
♥
VERY MUCH.

No...

I LOVE them TOO!

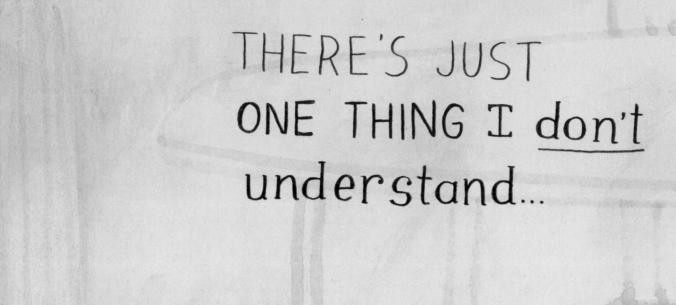

THERE'S JUST
ONE THING I _don't_
understand...

Why did they buy me
A COLLAR WITH THE
WRONG NAME ?